This Book
Belongs To:

....

....

FIVE-MINUTE TALES
for
FIVE
Year Olds

FIVE-MINUTE TALES
for
FIVE
Year Olds

A beautiful collection of original stories

p

Illustrated by Diana Catchpole

(Linda Rogers Associates)

Language consultant: Betty Root

This is a Parragon Publishing book
This edition published in 2005

Parragon Publishing
Queen Street House
4 Queen Street
BATH, BA1 1HE, UK

ISBN 1-40542-944-5

Printed in China

Contents

Daisy, the Detective

Jillian Harker

Daisy was six years old, and she knew that she wanted to be a detective. She had a little notebook and a magnifying glass. She carried them with her everywhere she went. When Daisy saw something interesting, she looked at it carefully through her magnifying glass. Then, she wrote notes in her book. Daisy liked mysteries, and she was always looking for clues.

"What are you doing, Daisy?" asked her little sister, Rose.

"I'm looking for clues, Rose," smiled Daisy.

"What's a clue?" asked Rose.

"Look!" said Daisy to her sister. She pointed to the soft earth underneath the rose bushes. "Can you see those footprints? Do you know what they are?"

"No, I don't!" answered her sister. "What are they?"

"Those are the footprints of a lion," said Daisy. "You can see where he walked across the yard. He must have escaped from the zoo."

"How do you know all this, Daisy?" asked Rose.

"I'm a detective," said Daisy. "I hunt for clues. Have you seen this?" Daisy pulled some fur from a thorn on one of the rose bushes. She held it out for her sister to see.

"Look!" said Daisy. "This is lion fur. The lion passed by here. He left his footprints in the soil as he crept by, and he caught his fur on that thorn. Next, he went over to the tree. He could be up there watching us right now."

"Wow!" said Daisy's sister.

Up in the tree, Daisy's cat, Ginger, was laying on a branch, licking a dirty paw. She heard Daisy's voice.

"Meow! Meow!" called Ginger, but Daisy didn't seem to notice.

"What other clues have you found, Daisy?" asked Rose.

"Look!" said Daisy to her sister. "Can you see that hole?"

"Where?" asked Rose.

"Right there," said Daisy, pointing at the flowerbed. "Someone has been digging. It must have been a band of pirates."

"Do you really think so?" asked Daisy's sister.

"Yes," said Daisy. "I'm a detective, and I know about these things. I hunt for clues. Look at this!"

Daisy picked up something from the ground near the hole. It was a big bone.

"The pirates left their treasure here years ago. Now, they've come back to collect it. They ate a meal here while they were digging. Perhaps they were still hard at work when we came along. They could be in the bushes watching us right now."

"Really?" asked Daisy's sister, shivering.

Daisy's dog, Rufus, was laying in the shade under a bush thinking about juicy bones. He heard Daisy talking.

"Woof! Woof!" barked Rufus.

But Daisy didn't seem
to notice.

Daisy saw some smoke coming from Mr. Brown's yard. It curled into the air high above the fence.

"Look!" Daisy said to her sister. "You see! There's another clue."

"What do you think it means?" asked Rose.

"It's a dragon, of course!" replied Daisy. "They breathe fire and smoke."

"Do you really think so?" asked Daisy's sister. Her eyes opened wide with fright.

"Yes, I do," said Daisy. "I'm a detective, and I know how to follow clues. Look at this!" Daisy pulled Rose toward the fence. They peeked through a crack between two boards. They could see flames and smoke in Mr. Brown's yard.

"Watch out!" yelled Daisy. "The dragon could be coming to get us."

"Ohhhh!" wailed her sister.

Mr. Brown lifted another forkful of leaves onto his bonfire. He heard Rose and Daisy talking behind the fence.

"Good morning, Daisy," said Mr. Brown. "How are you today?" But Daisy didn't seem to hear.

Just at that moment, Mom called out from the kitchen.

"Daisy! Rose! Could you come here a minute?" The two sisters ran across the yard to the back door.

"Guess what we've been doing, Mom!" said Rose. "We've been following clues all around the yard. Did you know that we've had a lion *and* pirates *and* a dragon in our yard?"

"Really?" said Mom. "Well, if you know all that, maybe you know something else as well. Do you know where the cookies have gone? There are none left in the container."

"Someone must have taken them," said Rose.

"But don't worry, Mom. Daisy can find out. Daisy is a brilliant detective. She will work it out." Rose turned to her sister.

"Do you know who did it, Daisy?" she asked.

Daisy didn't answer straight away. She slid her hand into her pocket.

"It's hard to say," mumbled Daisy. She half turned away from her mom and her sister, and then she pulled out her pocket. Secretly, Daisy shook a pile of crumbs onto the path. Then, she turned back to Rose and Mom, and smiled.

"I'm sorry," said Daisy. "I haven't got a clue."

The Trouble with Lionel

Jan Payne

Imagine a village filled with dragons riding around on bicycles, speeding around on skateboards, walking to school. The village would be filled with interesting dragons—and none would be more interesting than Lionel!

Lionel was only a small dragon, but he had a big problem. Each time he sneezed or coughed or laughed, flames would leap out of his mouth and set fire to everything around him.

Once, when he had a cold, Lionel sneezed and set fire to his tissue! And once, at the village fair, he laughed and set off all the fireworks at the same time!

Even Lionel's last birthday party was a
disaster. When he tried to blow out the candles on his
cake, the flames toasted the cake, burst the balloons,
set fire to the party hats, and melted all the ice cream.

Lionel's other dragon friends, Dipsy, Droopy, and
Donald, were able to control the amount of flames they
breathed out. They could light a match or a bonfire or
even cook the dinner. But poor Lionel could not.

"Try holding your breath," Dipsy advised him.

"Try keeping your mouth shut," was Droopy's helpful comment.

"I've got the perfect thing," said Donald, and he tied his favorite red and yellow scarf around Lionel's jaw.

"And don't you dare take it off!" he told Lionel.

"Just as you say, guys, just as you say," mumbled Lionel. For a while the scarf worked. And then, Lionel got an attack of the hiccups.

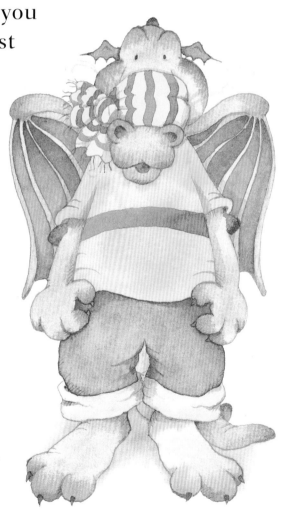

"Mmmm ... help! Mmmm ... aaaggghhh" gasped Lionel, trying to keep his lips together.

His friends tried everything. They even held him upside down while he drank a glass of water.

They fed him spoonfuls of sugar. They put ice cubes down his back.

But the hiccups just grew louder and louder and bigger and bigger. Then, everyone ran for cover when a huge wall of flame burst out of Lionel's mouth. In an instant, it burned down the village hall and scorched Mrs. Perkins' wash hanging out to dry three villages away.

"LIONEL!" shouted his friends.

"Sorry," wheezed Lionel. "But, hey guys, look on the bright side," he added. "The hiccups have stopped!"

From that day on, Lionel had to wear a special mouthpiece made out of fireproof material. The accidents stopped, and life in the dragon village settled down to normal.

Then, one day, the four friends were given a special job to do. One hundred miles away, a wicked witch had been frightening the local people. She put spells on their crops so that they got sick. She flew through the streets at night on her broomstick keeping everyone awake. She made the water in the wells taste terrible. And she turned the local cats and dogs into mice and toads.

Someone had to teach that witch a lesson!

For a whole week, the young dragons practiced their skills. All, that is, except Lionel. He wasn't allowed to practice.

When they were ready, the four young dragons took off, flying high above the fields and towns until they reached the village. There, they camped out in a huge cave and waited.

The next day, just as it was getting dark, the witch appeared. As she swept past them on her broomstick, her cloak billowed out around her. The shadow of her hat stood out in the evening sky.

The dragons watched the witch swoop over the village, chanting her magic spells. They knew they had to put a stop to the witch's tricks.

The next day, the four friends lay in wait for her. Dipsy saw her first. He shot out a tongue of flame, but it wasn't long enough.

Then Droopy aimed at her broomstick, but missed! Donald tried surrounding the witch with a circle of fire, but she flew right through the middle of it.

Backwards and forwards flew the witch, always just out of reach. As she flew, she gloated and chanted,

"Mud and slime and rotten smells,
I will use my magic spells
To turn you into hardboiled eggs
With sixteen arms and hairy legs."

The dragons didn't like the sound of that!

They quickly untied Lionel's mouthpiece.

"Go on, Lionel!" they cried.

Lionel took a deep breath and blew a huge flame up into the sky. It surrounded the witch's broomstick in an instant. The four friends watched as she fell, toppling over and over, until she finally landed upside down in a tree.

The dragons cheered loudly and shook each other by the hand. They gave Lionel a huge pat on the back.

When the dragons arrived back home, there was a lot of cheering. Lionel was a hero! And, believe it or not, he was able to celebrate, but this time without his mouthpiece.

You'll never guess why! Someone had found out that Lionel's favorite snack was coal! And, of course, the more coal he ate, the more flames of fire he produced. And his flames were becoming bigger and bigger!

So the answer to Lionel's embarrassing problem was ... EAT LESS COAL!!

It worked! And Lionel never had a problem with his flames ever again.

Well Really, Sam!

Jillian Harker

It was Tuesday morning at Rush Hill School. Mrs. Barton's class was sitting on the carpet, while she took attendance. When Mrs. Barton came to Sam's name, there was no answer—just silence. Suddenly, Marty's hand shot into the air.

"Mrs. Barton," he said, "as I was coming into school, I saw Sam playing with Mr. Pitt's dog." Mr. Pitt was the school janitor.

At that moment, the door flew open and in Sam rushed.

"You're late, Sam," Mrs Barton told him.

"You'll never guess what happened to me on the way to school this morning," said Sam, excitedly.

"Well really, Sam!" replied the teacher. "What?"

"You see, I was walking through the gate," began Sam, "when a huge monster leaped out of nowhere. It put its hairy hands on my shoulders, and pushed its slimy green face toward mine. I could feel its hot breath on my cheek, and ..." Sam paused.

"And?" asked Mrs. Barton.

"It poked out its gigantic tongue and licked me all over my face. Then, it ran off; I ran across the playground; and here I am," finished Sam.

"Sit down, Sam," said Mrs. Barton firmly. She marked

Sam late. "I think I'd better have a word with your mom," she muttered.

On Wednesday morning, when Mrs. Barton called the children onto the carpet, they were fidgeting.

"Settle down, now," she told them, opening her attendance book. When she got to Sam's name, there was no reply—just silence—and then a giggle. Alice's hand shot up.

"I know where Sam is," she said. "I saw him playing in the sandbox when I was walking across the playground."

Just then, the classroom door burst open and in ran Sam.

"You're late, Sam," Mrs. Barton greeted him.

"You'll never guess what happened to me on the way to school this morning," gasped Sam.

"Well really, Sam!" said Mrs. Barton. "What?"

"You see," said Sam, and the words tumbled out. "I was coming across the playground when, suddenly, the ground opened up and there was an enormous hole in front of me, and I couldn't stop in time, so I fell straight in and ..."

"And?" asked Mrs. Barton.

"I was at the bottom of this huge pit, with soil falling on top of me. I dug really fast to get myself out. Then, there was a rumble, and I was thrown out of the hole. It closed up behind me; and I ran across the playground; and here I am," finished Sam.

"Sit down, Sam!" ordered Mrs. Barton. She shook her head as she marked Sam late—again. "I really must talk to your mother," she muttered.

When Mrs. Barton took attendance on Thursday morning, the children were talking and looking round.

"Settle down, and face me," Mrs. Barton told them.

She began to read out their names. When she got to Sam's name, there was no reply—just silence, then lots of giggling. Becky's hand shot up.

"I know where Sam is," she said. "I saw him going into the candy store on his way to school."

Just then, the classroom door was flung open, and Sam crashed in.

"You're late, Sam," said Mrs. Barton.

"You'll never guess what happened to me on the way to school," said Sam, panting.

"Well really, Sam!" asked his teacher. "What?"

"You see, I was walking along the road," Sam said, his words pouring out, "when, suddenly, I felt myself being sucked toward this open door. I tried to pull away, but there was nothing I could do. It was an alien spaceship, and the aliens made me eat all this alien food before they let me go. Then, I ran all the way to school."

"Sit down, Sam," snapped Mrs. Barton, "and please ask your mother to come and see me tomorrow morning."

On Friday morning, when Mrs. Barton began to take attendance, several hands shot into the air. "Sam's not here," some children shouted. Mrs. Barton sighed loudly.

At that moment, Sam flung the door open.

"You'll never guess what happened this morning," he said, gasping. "There was a flood in our kitchen, and it was all my hamster's fault."

"Well really, Sam!" said Mrs. Barton. "That's quite enough of your stories. And I thought I told you to ask your mother to come and see me."

"Good afternoon, Mrs. Barton," said Sam's mom, poking her head around the door at lunchtime. "I'm sorry Sam was late this morning, but our hamster escaped last night. It got under the floorboards upstairs and chewed through the plastic water pipe. When we got up this morning, the whole kitchen was flooded."

"But it's cleared up now," smiled Sam, "and I won't be late again. I think I've had enough adventures."

"Really, Sam?" grinned Mrs. Barton. "So have I!"

Lost in the Snow

Nick Ellsworth

Billy and Bobby were two sheepdogs. They lived on a farm up in the hills. Their job was to help the farmer, Joe Kinley, bring the sheep safely in from the fields.

Early in the morning on Christmas Eve, the two dogs woke up in their basket.

"It's very cold this morning," shivered Billy, nestling deeper into his blanket.

"I think it might snow," said Bobby, looking out the window at the gray sky.

Joe came into the kitchen, rubbing his hands together.

"Brrr … it's frosty this morning, boys," he said, putting the kettle on to make a cup of tea.

After breakfast, the dogs ran around trying to keep warm, while Joe cleaned the house. He wanted everything to look neat and clean for Christmas Day. As he was cleaning the living room fireplace, he suddenly remembered something.

"Oh, no! I've forgotten to chop down my Christmas tree!" he exclaimed. "I'd better go and get one right away."

The Christmas trees grew in a valley on the other side of the hill. It would take Joe all afternoon to walk there and back.

"You'll have to bring the sheep in on your own today," he told Billy and Bobby. "I'll see you back here this evening."

Joe gave each dog a pat, put on his warmest jacket, and stepped out into the yard with Billy and Bobby following close behind him.

As the dogs left to bring in the sheep, the snow started to fall quite heavily.

"This snow's going to make it a lot harder to round up the sheep," thought Bobby.

The two sheepdogs trotted up the lane and then started to cross some small fields. Finally, they reached the big field where the sheep were huddled together.

As the dogs made their way up a steep slope, Bobby heard a startled yelp behind him.

Looking around, he saw that Billy had stumbled into an icy hole. He seemed to have hurt his front leg.

"Are you hurt badly?" Bobby asked, feeling worried.

"I don't think I can walk," said Billy quietly, struggling through the snow.

Bobby helped his friend over to a nearby tree.

"You sit and rest here," he said. "I'll take the sheep quickly to the farm and come back to help you as soon as I can."

After making Billy as comfortable as he could, Bobby began to round up the sheep. It was extremely hard work without Billy's help. By the time he'd managed to get the sheep out of the field and onto the lane, Bobby felt very tired.

He guided the sheep back to the farm and put them into their pen. After a few slurps of water, Bobby headed back to the field where he had left Billy.

It was almost dark when Bobby got to the spot where he'd left Billy, and it was growing colder by the minute. When he reached the tree, he was surprised to see that Billy wasn't there any more.

"Perhaps he's limped off to try and find help," thought Bobby, searching the ground for footprints. But the freshly falling snow had covered any tracks that Billy might have left.

Bobby sniffed around, trying to pick up Billy's scent. But again, the new snow had covered up any smell of him.

Bobby barked loudly into the darkness, hoping to hear Billy bark back. But all he heard was the whistle of the wind through the trees. Then, he had a frightening thought.

"Maybe Billy fell asleep and was buried by the falling snow!"

He began to dig frantically in the snow around the tree, but all he found was the wet grass beneath. Poor Billy seemed to have disappeared into thin air.

Bobby realized that
he needed to get more help, so he
decided to go back and get Joe. He
plodded wearily across the snow-covered fields
and then along the lane that led to the farm.
Finally, Bobby reached the farm. By this time, he
felt so exhausted he could hardly walk through the
kitchen door.

"There you are, Bobby!" said Joe, when he saw the tired
dog come in. "We were getting really worried about you."

In the middle of the kitchen, Bobby saw a brightly lit Christmas tree covered with sparkling decorations. Beneath it, sitting in a basket by the fire, was Billy. He had a bandage around his injured leg.

"Am I glad to see you!" said Billy, grinning up at him.

"Thank goodness you're safe," said Bobby with relief. "But how did you get back?"

Billy explained that Joe had found him in the field on his way back from cutting the Christmas tree. Somehow, he'd managed to carry Billy and the tree all the way back to the farm.

As they drifted off to sleep that night, Bobby and Billy had already forgotten about their eventful day. They were both looking forward to the excitement that the morning would bring. For tomorrow would be Christmas Day!

Poppy's Fairy Godmother

Jan Payne

Poppy pressed her face up against the shop window. "Oh," she sighed, "it's beautiful!"

"And look at the ballet shoes," said her sister, Katie.

Poppy was looking at the prettiest ballet dress she had ever seen. It was made of white lace with white satin straps. The ballet shoes were pink satin. Poppy had just started ballet lessons, and she wanted the dress and shoes more than anything in the whole world.

"They're fab!" she said to Katie. "Just fab!" "Fab" was a new word for Poppy. Her older sister, Katie, used it all the time. "Do you think Mom would let me have them?" she asked.

"I don't know, Pops," said Katie. "You could ask and see what she says."

When Poppy got home she asked Mom about the ballet dress and shoes. She described the pure white lace, the satin straps, and the dainty shoes.

"You should see them, Mom," said Poppy. "They're fab!"

"I'm sure they are, Poppy," said Mom, "but I just can't afford to buy them at the moment. Maybe in a few months."

"A few months isn't long to wait," said Dad, when he saw Poppy's disappointed face. "Otherwise," he added jokingly, "you find yourself a fairy godmother."

"Like Cinderella, you mean?" asked Poppy, her eyes sparkling.

"Exactly—like Cinderella," smiled Dad.

Poppy thought this was a brilliant idea. But how could she find a fairy godmother?

"I know," she said to Katie, "I'll send a note up the chimney. It always works at Christmas."

Katie agreed to help Poppy write her note.

"Fairy Godmother wanted. Someone kind to help a ballet dancer. Poppy Perez, aged 6."

Then, Katie sent the note up the chimney.

Poppy was sure it would work. "I'll know my fairy godmother when she comes," she said to Katie. "She'll be beautiful, with a long white dress and wings."

The following week, Aunt Dolly came to stay.

Aunt Dolly was Poppy's favorite aunt. She was pretty and kind and funny. She read Poppy stories at bedtime. She took her to the park, and she made clothes for Poppy's favorite doll. Poppy loved her.

"But there's no way she's my fairy godmother," said Poppy to Katie. "Not with a name like Dolly ... no way!"

Poppy started to look at people for telltale signs like wings hidden beneath a coat or a sparkling tiara in a shopping bag, or a magic wand in a pocket.

Grandpa came for lunch that weekend. Of course, it couldn't be him! That would be a joke. Fairy godmothers aren't men! Nor could it be Mrs. Jenkins, who lived next door. Although, she did have a sweet smile.

No, Poppy was prepared to be patient. Her fairy godmother would come. She was sure of it.

The next day, Poppy walked into the kitchen and Mom was ironing a long white dress!

"Oh," said Poppy, "that's lovely!"

"Yes, isn't it," said Mom, smiling.

While Poppy was playing in
the yard, she happened to look
through the window of the garden
shed. Grandpa was in there, and he
was sticking
glitter onto
what looked like
a pair of white wings!

"Oh!" said Poppy to herself.
Later in the day, she saw
Mrs. Jenkins cycling back from
the stores. She had a wand
sticking out of the basket on
the front of her bicycle!
"What's going on?"
thought Poppy. It was all
very mysterious.

The days passed by slowly, and still Poppy's fairy godmother hadn't appeared. Doubts began to creep into Poppy's mind. Perhaps she wouldn't come after all?

"What's more," she said sadly to Katie, "the ballet dress and pink shoes aren't in the store window. Somebody else must have bought them."

"If they have, don't worry," said Katie. "There'll be others, you'll see."

A few evenings later, Poppy was going upstairs to bed.

"Please, will you come and read to me, Aunt Dolly?" she asked.

"Of course," said Aunt Dolly. "Give me five minutes."

When Aunt Dolly came into Poppy's bedroom, Poppy had the surprise of her life. Aunt Dolly was wearing a long white dress! She wore a pair of sparkling white wings behind her shoulders, and she was carrying a silver wand!

"Aunt Dolly," breathed Poppy, her eyes shining, "you look beautiful."

"I have something for you," smiled Aunt Dolly. And she gave Poppy a box wrapped in pink tissue paper.

Inside were the ballet dress and pink shoes!

"*You* are my fairy godmother!" laughed Poppy, leaping out of bed and kissing her aunt.

Aunt Dolly hugged her. Poppy put on the dress and shoes. They fit perfectly. When she went downstairs, Mom, Dad, and Katie were all waiting with smiling faces. Mom told Poppy that Aunt Dolly was going to a costume party, which explained why Mom had been ironing the dress and Grandpa had been making the wings.

"How fab!" laughed Poppy. "So, real people can be fairy godmothers, too!"

There's No Such Thing as Magic!

Jillian Harker

Lucy Wilson had sandy-colored hair and freckles. So did her older brother, Mark. They looked so much alike that people sometimes thought they were twins. Lucy and Mark liked doing the same things, too. They loved jigsaw puzzles and books, kicking a ball around their big back lawn, and building forts from old boxes.

But in one way Lucy and Mark were very different.

Lucy believed in magic. She believed that fairies lived at the end of the yard and that you could make a wish on a rainbow. She believed in spells and magic words. Mark thought she was crazy.

"There's no such thing as magic!" he said. "It's just a load of rubbish. I don't believe in magic."

"Please yourself," answered Lucy. "You'll change your mind."

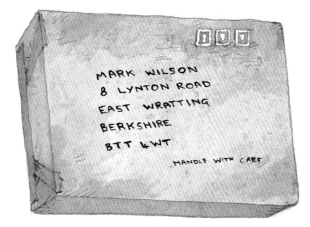

The next day was Mark's seventh birthday. Along with Mark's cards, the postman brought a large box. Mark's name was written in big writing in black ink on the front.

"It's from Auntie Sadie!" yelled Mark, full of excitement. Auntie Sadie always sent interesting presents. With a huge grin on his face, Mark tore open the parcel. The grin quickly disappeared.

"The Box of Tricks—A First Magic Kit," he said, reading the bottom of the box. A look of disappointment spread across Mark's face. Lucy pulled the top off the box, peeked inside, and took out a folded piece of black cloth. She shook it out.

"A magician's cape!" she gasped. She swirled the cape around. Inside the black cloth, the cape was lined with bright red silk.

"Wow!" yelled Lucy. "Look! There's a wand and a pot of magic powder, too! You could do any magic you wanted to with this."

"Rubbish!" snapped Mark. "There's no such thing as magic!" And he began to open his birthday cards.

The rest of the day was very busy. Mark's friends were coming, and there was food to prepare, balloons to blow up, and party bags to fill. Mark didn't look at the magic kit again, but Lucy did.

While everyone was busy, she slipped the cape around her shoulders, picked up the wand, and practiced saying magic words. She held up the little glass pot of shiny, silver magic powder and wished she could think of some special magic to do.

After the party, when his friends had left, Mark suddenly asked, "Has anyone seen Footsie? I can't remember seeing her all day." Footsie was Mark's cat. She was mostly black, but she had four pure white paws. Mark loved her very much. No one could remember seeing Footsie.

"Don't worry," said Mom. "She'll be back soon. Maybe all the noise frightened her away."

But Footsie didn't come back. Even when it grew dark and Dad stood in the yard calling her name over and over again, Footsie didn't appear.

The next morning, Mark got up early. There was still no sign of Footsie. He asked Mrs. Thomas next door if she had seen Footsie, but she hadn't. By the end of the day, Mark was very worried. Then, Lucy pulled him into the sitting room. She handed him the magic box.

"We'll just have to do some magic," she told him. "That'll bring her back."

"Don't be silly, Lucy," said Mark angrily. "There's no such thing as magic!"

"Yes, there is!" replied Lucy, throwing the cloak around herself. "I'll show you!" She picked up the magic wand, waved it in the air, and sang in a singsong voice:

"We miss Footsie's quiet purr,
her four white paws and silky fur,
fur that's soft and darkest black,
I wish for Footsie to come back."

"What are you doing?" Mark asked, as Lucy rushed into the kitchen with the small glass bottle. "This will never work."

Lucy didn't listen. She filled Footsie's dish with food and put it by the back door near the cat flap.

Then, she sprinkled magic powder all around it.

"You'll see," she said.

Mark woke early again the next morning. Lucy had gone

to the kitchen before him. Footsie's bowl was empty, but there was no sign of Footsie.

"How does your special magic powder help now?" sniffed Mark.

"Easy!" smiled his sister. "Look, Footsie's been back, hasn't she? And now I know how to find her." She opened the back door and pointed at the walkway. A set of silvery footprints led away from the house.

"Of course!" yelled Mark. "We've just got to follow these." He rushed down the walkway, following the shiny footprints. They led him to the end of the yard and around the back of the shed.

From a hollow under the hedge, Mark heard a soft purring noise.

"See!" said Lucy. "I told you magic works. Here's Footsie."

Mark bent down.

"There's no such thing as …" he began. He didn't finish. He turned to Lucy and pulled her down to look. There, in the hollow, lay Footsie and four perfect little kittens.

"Magic!" whispered Mark. And Lucy grinned.

The Lion Who Couldn't Roar

Nick Ellsworth

*T*oby, the lion cub, had a problem. The first time he opened his mouth to roar all that came out was a squeak! Try as he might, he just couldn't give a lion-like ROAARR! Poor Toby didn't know what to do. Things became even worse when all the other cubs began to laugh at him.

"Perhaps I'm not a lion at all," thought Toby sadly, and wandered off into the jungle. He was feeling sorry for himself.

After a while, Toby stopped for a rest. Nearby, a small group of mice were playing around under a leafy bush.

Toby usually liked to chase mice, but he felt so unhappy, he just couldn't be bothered.

"Look, a lion!" squeaked one mouse.

The mice were scared of lions and began to run away.

"I'm not going to hurt you," pleaded Toby. "I'm a mouse too. Listen."

Toby opened his mouth and out came a little squeak.

"Can I stay with you, please?" he asked. "I haven't anyhere else to go."

All the mice huddled together, and after a while the biggest mouse said,

"You must be a mouse to squeak like that. We'd be very happy for you to stay with us."

So, Toby followed the mice into the jungle.

A little while later, the biggest mouse stopped very still and sniffed the air.

"I smell elephants," he said. "And they're very near."

"What shall we do?" cried the smallest mouse. He was very frightened.

"Run!" yelled the biggest mouse.

Toby and the mice ran off as fast as their legs could carry them. But, as Toby was so much bigger than the mice, he almost trampled them under his feet.

"Be careful, Toby!" shouted the biggest mouse. "You're going to flatten us all!"

Soon they stopped running, and the biggest mouse sniffed the air again.

"All clear," he said. "Okay, let's get some food."

The mice collected all the berries they could find and put them in a big heap for everyone to share. But Toby thought that the berries were meant for him, and he swallowed them all in one big gulp.

"Mmm, delicious," he said, licking his lips.

"Those berries were meant for all of us," said the biggest mouse, grumpily.

"Sorry!" said Toby. The mice then collected lots of grass and twigs, which they made into a little house. But, when Toby tried to go inside it, he was far too big to fit in, and the whole thing came crashing down.

"You've destroyed our house; you've eaten all our food; and you've almost trampled us," said the biggest mouse, angrily. " We want you to leave ... right now!"

Toby began to walk away slowly with his tail between his legs. He felt very sad.

"What am I going to do?" he thought.

Just then, he heard a voice behind him. "Hey, you! Wait a minute!"

It was one of the mice.

"Look!" said Mouse kindly. "You're not a mouse. You're a lion."

"But, I squeak like a mouse," said Toby sadly.

"Don't you worry about that," said Mouse. "I'll help you get your roar."

Mouse jumped into a puddle and splashed Toby with muddy water. Toby tried to roar, but all that came out was a tiny squeak.

Squeak!

Next, Mouse jumped onto Toby's back and began to pull his ears. All Toby could manage was another tiny squeak.

Finally, Mouse shouted at him. "You're the stupidest lion I've ever seen!"

This time, Toby was really angry. He opened his mouth and let out a great big SQUEAK.

"Hmm," said Mouse.

He did not know what to do next to help Toby, so Mouse decided to go for a refreshing swim in the river.

Toby sat at the water's edge, wondering if he'd ever be able to roar.

Suddenly, out of the corner of his eye, he noticed large crocodiles swimming toward Mouse with their mouths wide open.

Toby leaped to his feet and tried to warn Mouse, but all that came out was a squeak! He ran around and waved his paws, but Mouse still didn't see him.

The crocodiles were swimming closer to poor Mouse.

"This is my final chance," thought Toby. He opened his mouth again, took a great big breath, and out came a huge and terrifying ... ROAAAAAAR!!!

When they heard the terrible sound of a roaring lion, the frightened crocodiles swam away quickly .

Mouse swam back and shook the water from his fur.

"You see," he said to Toby with a grin. "I told you I'd make you roar."

Toby and Mouse are now great friends. Toby went back to play with the other lion cubs. He became a very happy lion, but he never forgot about the mouse who taught him to roar.

The Ugly Princess

Jan Payne

Princess Cressida lived in a magnificent palace in a faraway land. The princess had no idea that she was very beautiful. Whenever she looked at herself in the mirror, she saw someone who seemed to be extremely ugly.

"How ugly I am!" she would sigh to herself. "No one has ever looked as ugly as I do."

Princess Cressida's parents, King Otto and Queen Beatrice, were very strict. They knew their daughter was the most beautiful girl in the land, but they didn't want her to know that.

The king and queen were worried that their daughter might become very vain. So, they took away all the mirrors from the palace except one. This mirror was in the princess' bedroom, and it was a trick mirror, like the ones you can find at carnivals. So, whenever Princess Cressida looked in the mirror, she saw someone who looked quite ugly. The princess was a sweet and cheerful girl, so she didn't worry about the way she looked. She was kind and gentle, and everyone who met her loved her.

The king and queen were also strict about where Princess Cressida was allowed to go. So, she either stayed in the palace or walked around its huge, wild gardens.

Princess Cressida loved to walk through the gardens. Her dog, Goldie, always came with her, rushing along at the princess' side. One afternoon, she set off on a walk as usual. She was wearing a long dress made of crimson silk, and her golden hair fell loosely down her back. Princess Cressida had no idea how lovely she looked. Earlier, when she had looked in the mirror, she had seen her usual ugly reflection.

"I would so love to be pretty," she said to Goldie, stroking his soft golden head. "But I'm not and never will be, so that's that! I'm not going to think about it again."

It was a lovely day. As the princess walked through the palace grounds, she gazed at the brightly colored flowers and leafy trees. She noticed the beautiful blue sky with hardly a cloud in it and the pretty birds flying above her. In fact, she was so busy looking at all the beautiful things around her, that she didn't realize she had walked out of the gardens and into the nearby town.

While Princess Cressida walked
down the street, a crowd of townspeople
began to gather around her. She noticed
they were staring at her.

"What is wrong?" she called out in a
trembling voice. But the people said nothing and
went on staring at her.

The princess hurried on. More people stopped to look at her. Some whispered to each other when they saw her, and two young men bowed as she passed them. A little further on, another man took off his cloak and laid it on the ground for her to walk on.

Princess Cressida was confused and embarrassed.

"Why is everyone behaving like this?" she asked herself. "They are teasing me! I expect they're staring at me because they can't believe that anyone can be so ugly," she sighed.

The princess was almost in tears as she ran away from the crowd into a nearby building. It was dark inside, but she could just make out a room with a small window. Sitting at a table was a young man with his head in his hands. His back was bent in a funny shape, and his clothes were rags. When the young man raised his head, she could see that he was very ugly. He turned away so that the princess could not see his face.

"Please don't look at me!" he cried out.

Princess Cressida felt great pity for him. She held out her hand toward him. "Don't hide your face," she said gently. "The way you look means nothing to me."

The young man looked at her. Although his face was very ugly, his eyes were warm and kind.

"Thank you," said the young man. "No one as beautiful as you has ever spoken so kindly to me before." And he took her outstretched hand in his.

"Me ... beautiful?" asked Princess Cressida. She was even more surprised at what happened next. As the young man's hand touched her own, he was instantly changed into a tall and handsome prince.

And that was how Princess Cressida learned about her true appearance. She and the prince fell in love at that moment. He told her how a spell had been cast over

him at birth, which would only be broken when a beautiful princess was kind to him.

At Princess Cressida's wedding, King Otto and Queen Beatrice asked their daughter to forgive them for their strict and unkind behavior. And, of course, she did. If it hadn't been for her parents, she never would have met her very own Prince Charming!

I Want to Sing!

Nicola Baxter

Twitter! Grrrrr! Ooo oooo! Sssssss! Ee ee!

It is not quiet in the jungle. Hidden among the leaves, the jungle friends are calling and chatting to each other all day long.

It was a typical noisy morning when Snake had a good idea. He was coiled around a branch, enjoying the warm sunshine. Snake told his idea to a nearby toucan, who was busy cracking nuts on a branch below Snake's head.

Toucan listened carefully, before putting her head to one side and blinking her bright eyes.

"That's a good idea!" she chirped. "In fact, that's a REALLY GOOD IDEA! I'm going to tell the other animals!"

Now toucans are a lot more talkative than snakes. So, very soon all the birds and other animals on all the nearby trees knew about Snake's idea. Even Crocodile, who was slithering around in the dark waters below, knew about it.

What was the idea? Snake had suggested starting up a jungle band. Why had no one thought of it before? There would be no more horrible, loud screeching noices coming out of the jungle. Instead, there would be the sweet sound of music.

Everyone wanted to be in the band. In a surprisingly short time, the jungle animals had chosen a song and started to rehearse.

The result was amazing. After years and years of chatting away in the noisy jungle all day long, the animals were really good at listening to each other. By midday, they sounded as if they had been singing together for years.

"Oooo-oo, oooo-oo!" sang the toucans.

"Snappity, snappity-snap!" went Crocodile, tapping on a tree stump with his big, strong jaws.

"Hissss, ssss, hissss, ssss!" hissed Snake, as he wrapped himself around a nearby branch.

"Ee-ee-oo-oo! Ee-ee-oo-oo!" yelled the monkeys, swinging by their tails in time to the music.

"We sound gr-e-e-at!" said Snake.

"One more time!" called the biggest toucan.

"A-one, a-two, a-three, four, five …!"

Oooo-oo, oooo-oo! Hissss, ssss, hissss, ssss!
Ee-ee-oo-oo! Ee-ee-oo-oo! Snappity, snappity-snap!

The song sounded nearly perfect, and the animals had almost reached the end when … SQUAAAAAAWK!

"What was that noise?" asked the biggest toucan.

"Er … let's do that again," he suggested. "A-one, a-two, a-three, four, five …!"

The animals started to sing, and once again, they had almost finished the song when … SQUAAAAAAWK!

All the animals turned their heads. Suddenly, three tiny hummingbirds swooped down and lifted up a large leaf. Behind it, not looking at all embarrassed, sat a large parrot. "Squaaaaawk!" she said cheerfully.

The biggest toucan took charge again. "I see we have a new member of the band. I wonder if I could ask you to sing a little more quietly, especially at the end?"

"I thought your song needed a really BIG finish," replied the parrot. "I can sing it louder, if you like. Listen! SQUAAAAAAAAAWK!"

"NOOO!" cried the toucans and the monkeys and the hummingbirds and Snake and Crocodile.

"Let's try it again," said the biggest toucan. "And this time, Parrot, perhaps you could sing along in the middle and just ... er ... waggle your wings at the end."

Parrot nodded enthusiastically. The biggest toucan counted them in. "A-one, a-two, a-three, four, five ...!"

Oooo-oo, oooo-oo! Hissss, ssss, hissss, ssss! Squawk, squawk! Ee-ee-oo-oo! Ee-ee-oo-oo! Snappity, snappity-snap! Squaaaawk!

"Sorry!" squawked Parrot. "That noise at the end was me." She had waggled her wings too eagerly and fallen off her perch.

"Allow me," snarled Crocodile, who began to slither toward the fluttering parrot.

"No! No! There's no need for that!" cried the biggest toucan. He was afraid that Crocodile was going to take matters into his own claws (or, rather, his own jaws!).

"Let's not have the squawking all the way through ... or the waggling at the end," suggested the biggest toucan.

"But I want to sing!" cried Parrot.

" Well ... perhaps ... you should simply waggle your wings a bit less!" replied the toucan.

"Let's try that one more time. A-one, a-two, a-three, four, five ...!"

Oooo-oo, oooo-oo! Hissss, ssss, hissss, ssss! Ee-ee-oo-oo! Ee-ee-oo-oo! Snappity-snap! Squaaaawk! Squaaaawk!

It was terrible!

"I got a bit carried away at the end," explained Parrot. "I can't help joining in. And anyway, the song does need to have a BIG ending."

"What it needs ..." snapped Crocodile in a very low voice, but before he could finish ...

"I've got it!" whooped the biggest toucan. "I think I've got the answer!"

Squaaaaawk!
Squaaaawk!

"Every band needs to have a conductor so why can't Parrot be OUR conductor? After all, she certainly knows how to waggle her wings!"

"But I want to sing!" squawked Parrot.

"I think it's a s-s-splendid idea!" hissed Snake.

"I suppose I could try if you REALLY think I can do it," replied Parrot.

"You can! You can!" chorused the animals.

"Ready, then ... here goes! A-one, a-five, a-seven, three, six ...!" called Parrot.

These days, the air is filled with the beautiful music of the jungle band. And you only hear a small squawk from a busy parrot every now and then!

Wills, the Wizard

Tony Payne

Wills had six brothers, and they were all older than him. Strangely, Wills' dad also had six brothers who were also older than he was. Wills' mom said that the seventh son of a seventh son was always a very clever wizard.

Mom only said it as a joke, but Wills believed her even though he couldn't do magic—and he was only six years old.

Wills was really excited to think that he was a real wizard. He told all his brothers and all his uncles *and* all his friends, but they just smiled and didn't believe him one bit. They laughed and said, "Of course you are!" but they didn't believe him.

Every Tuesday afternoon at school, Wills' class did drawing and painting and cutting things out. One Tuesday, Wills made a tall pointy hat out of black card. He glued on lots of shiny stars and added a streak of lightning in silver foil, too.

The hat looked really good, but when Wills put it on, the hat came right down to his nose. He had to cut out two round holes to see where he was going.

"Never mind!" thought Wills. Next, he made a wand from a stick and another shiny star. It was great! It looked as if it would really work—as if powerful magic was bottled up inside, itching to get out and do something amazing.

Suddenly, the star on the end fell off. Wills was not going to be beaten. He simply stuck the star back on with stronger glue.

Wills practiced waving his wand for hours. He didn't want magic to happen accidentally because he hadn't waved it correctly.

Sometimes, Wills held out the wand in front of him like a sword.

Other times, he lifted one hand high above his head, like a dancer, and held the wand stretched out in front of his body.

Wills' friends teased him, asking him when they could see some real magic. Wills knew they didn't believe he was a wizard. He did think, briefly, of turning his best friend, John, into a toad just to see the look on the faces of his friends.

But no, that was not how a wizard should behave. And yet, it wouldn't do any harm to practice turning things into toads, would it? It might come in handy one day when he needed a toad assistant.

Wills and his friends looked around for something that no one would miss. They found an old pail with a hole in it. That would do.

Looking like a knight, Wills gracefully passed his wand over the pail. "Abracadabra!" he cried. It was the only magic word he knew. The pail did not change. His friends laughed.

Wills' friends laughed again when he tried to turn a stop sign into a giant ice cream and a tree trunk into chocolate pudding. Wills began to feel disappointed that his magic hadn't worked … yet!

There was a school field trip the next day. Miss Green, Wills' teacher, took the whole class out to the nearby woods. Wills had left his pointy hat and wand behind. He was tired of everyone laughing at him when he wore his wizard's hat and carried his wand. People who were not wizards just didn't understand.

When the children had been in the woods for a while, they heard a loud crackling sound and noticed the strong smell of smoke. It was a forest fire! The children could see fierce flames blowing toward some houses at the edge of the woods.

"Oh no!" cried Wills' friend, John. "My house is over there! It'll be all burned down!" Then, Miss Green said that her house was nearby, too.

She gathered up the children and led them away from any danger, but she was really worried about her own house. Wills could definitely tell.

"What a shame I haven't got my wand!" he said to John, who was walking along next to him. "I could have pointed it like this," said Wills, taking up his knight's pose and pointing a very small finger up at the sky. "And I could have said, um ... HOT DOGS AND CUPCAKES!"

As he said these words, a huge bolt of lightning flew from Wills' finger up into the sky. The thunder was so loud that it knocked everyone off their feet. Then, it rumbled on.

Finally, the thunder grew quieter and quieter, until it fizzled out altogether. Wills looked at his finger in amazement, then a huge grin spread slowly over his face.

"Or I could just point my finger like this," he yelled, "and say PEANUT BUTTER AND MACARONI!"

This time the lightning streak was even brighter, and the thunder even louder. Then, Wills used both hands and yelled anything that came into his head.

There was a huge streak of lightning in the sky, followed by a large rumble of thunder. The sky darkened, and soon, rain was pouring down where the fire was burning. Where the children stood, it was still dry and sunny. Everyone was cheering Wills. They were truly amazed by his magic.

Wills had put out the fire and saved the houses. He hadn't needed his hat and wand after all, or any of his magic words. The magic power was all in him ... Wills.

Wills, the hero.

WILLS ... THE WIZARD!